All About Masks

Debbie Croft

Contents

Masks	2
Why Masks Are Worn	4
Masks from All Over the World	8
Masks Worn on Stage	12
Chinese Masks	14
Japanese Masks	16
Inuit Masks	20
Masks Then and Now	22
Glossary	24

Masks

Masks are covers that people wear over their faces.

Some masks only cover part of the face,
but other masks cover all of the face.

Many masks have small holes at each side
with strings tied onto them.

People place the masks over their faces,
and tie the strings into a bow behind their heads.
The masks do not fall off when people move around.

Why Masks Are Worn

Sometimes, people wear masks
to hide their faces in a play or a parade.
They wear the masks
because they are pretending
to be someone else.

People wear masks for fun
at parties or fairs, too.
The masks are very colourful.

Some people wear masks
to protect their faces and to keep themselves safe.

Doctors and dentists wear face masks
so they do not spread germs to their **patients**.

Masks are often worn by rescue workers. Sometimes, they have to help people who have been in an **accident**, and there is a lot of dust or smoke in the air. The masks help to stop rescue workers from breathing in the dust and smoke.

Some people who play sport wear masks. Masks can protect their face and teeth in games, such as softball and ice hockey.

Firefighters wear masks to stop them from breathing in smoke.

Ice hockey players wear masks to protect their faces.

Masks from All Over the World

Masks have been worn all over the world for thousands of years.

The first masks were made from animal skins, clay and paper.

an old African mask made from wood, leather and shells

8

Many masks made years ago were the same shape.
But they did not always look the same,
because animal teeth, hair, bones, paint,
shells and feathers were put on them, too.

an old mask from the Torres Strait Islands, Australia

Many masks were used by groups of dancers in their villages.

The dancers used the masks to tell stories about people and their families who had lived in years gone by.

Think and Talk About …
Today, many masks are made from leather, metal, cloth and plastic.

Dancers use masks to tell stories about people from long ago.

Masks Worn on Stage

Long, long ago, people wore masks when they were in a play on the stage.

Each actor would **pretend** to be someone else.

Today, people still wear masks
to hide their faces in plays,
and in movies and television shows.

Actors on stage sometimes wear masks and pretend to be other people.

Chinese Masks

In many countries, there are huge parades for the Chinese New Year.
At this time, many people wear masks that have lots of bright colours.

People think red is a really lucky colour, so many people wear masks that have red decorations.

Japanese Masks

In some Japanese plays, actors dress in beautiful clothes when they are on the stage.

All the **actors** in the play are men, so sometimes a man has to wear a mask and pretend to be a woman.

> **Think and Talk About …**
> Actors sometimes use a fan as a prop when they are on stage.

Japanese actors sometimes wear masks and dress in beautiful clothes.

Japanese masks are very **plain**.
They are made from wood and have holes
for the eyes, nose and mouth.
The masks are sometimes painted in bright colours.

The men who wear these masks must be clever actors.
They have to help the people who are watching the play
understand the story.

Inuit Masks

Inuit people from Greenland, Canada
and the United States of America wear masks, too.
Their masks are often worn during parades,
when lots of people tell stories and sing songs.

Inuit masks are made from wood, animal skins,
bones and feathers.
People sometimes use metal tools
to make patterns on the masks.

Masks Then and Now

Masks have been worn by people all around the world. They are worn by dancers and actors to tell stories of long ago.

Today, many people have to wear masks for their work or when playing sport, to protect themselves from danger. People like to wear masks at parades and parties, too.

Doctors wear masks so they do not spread germs to their patients.

Baseball players and builders wear masks to protect their faces.

23

Glossary

accident (*noun*) an event that happens by chance

actors (*noun*) people who act on a stage or in a film

patients (*noun*) people who are checked by a doctor or a dentist

plain (*adjective*) something that is very simple

pretend (*verb*) to make believe that something is true